Want to Bet?

"**Y**ou win too much," Gloria said.

She sat down on the grass and thought.

I sat down too. I wondered what was on her mind.

"Well," Gloria said, "I guess you can win at *ordinary* things. But I can do something special."

"Like what?" I said.

"Bet you I can move the sun," she said.

Julian, Huey, and Gloria books by Ann Cameron

The Stories Julian Tells

More Stories Julian Tells

Julian's Glorious Summer

Julian, Secret Agent

Julian, Dream Doctor

The Stories Huey Tells

More Stories Huey Tells

Gloria Rising

More Stories Julian Tells

by Ann Cameron
illustrated by Ann Strugnell

A STEPPING STONE BOOK™
Random House 🏠 New York

Text copyright © 1986 by Ann Cameron. Illustrations copyright © 1986 by Ann Strugnell.

All rights reserved. Published in the United States by Random House Children's Books, a division of Random House, Inc., New York. Originally published by Alfred A. Knopf, an imprint of Random House Children's Books, a division of Random House, Inc., New York, in 1986.

RANDOM HOUSE and colophon are registered trademarks and A STEPPING STONE BOOK and colophon are trademarks of Random House, Inc.

www.randomhouse.com/kids
www.steppingstonesbooks.com

Educators and librarians, for a variety of teaching tools, visit us at
www.randomhouse.com/teachers

Cover illustration copyright © Robert Papp

Library of Congress Cataloging-in-Publication Data
Cameron, Ann.
More stories Julian tells / by Ann Cameron ; illustrated by Ann Strugnell.
  p.   cm. — "A Stepping Stone book."
SUMMARY: More episodes in the life of Julian, including a bet with his best friend Gloria, a secret project, and what happens when his brother Huey decides to be Superboy.
ISBN 978-0-394-82454-3 (trade) — ISBN 978-0-394-96969-5 (lib. bdg.)
[1. Family life—Fiction. 2. Friendship—Fiction. 3. African Americans—Fiction.]
I. Strugnell, Ann, ill. II. Title.
PZ7.C1427Mo 2006 [Fic]—dc22 2005036385

Printed in the United States of America 49

For Rosalie Grossman, whose insight, wit, sympathy, and faith helped me around the curves in my river—A.C.

Contents

A Day When Frogs Wear Shoes   3

The Bet   21

I Learn Firefighting   32

    I Wish for Smokey the Bear   32

    Superboy and Me   44

    Huey Makes the Leap   49

The Box   53

A Curve in the River   68

More Stories
Julian Tells

A DAY
WHEN FROGS
WEAR SHOES

My little brother, Huey, my best friend,
Gloria, and I were sitting on our front steps.
It was one of those hot summer days when

everything stands still. We didn't know what to do. We were watching the grass grow. It didn't grow fast.

"You know something?" Gloria said. "This is a slow day."

"It's so slow the dogs don't bark," Huey said.

"It's so slow the flies don't fly," Gloria said.

"It's so slow ice cream wouldn't melt," I said.

"If we had any ice cream," Huey said.

"But we don't," Gloria said.

We watched the grass some more.

"We better do something," I said.

"Like what?" Gloria asked.

"We could go visit Dad," Huey said.

"That's a *terrible* idea," I said.

"Why?" Huey asked. "I like visiting Dad."

My father has a shop about a mile from our house, where he fixes cars. Usually it is fun to visit him. If he has customers, he always introduces us as if we were important guests. If he doesn't have company, sometimes he lets us ride in the cars he puts up on the lift. Sometimes he buys us treats.

"Huey," I said, "usually, visiting Dad is a good idea. Today, it's a dangerous idea."

"Why?" Gloria said.

"Because we're bored," I said. "My dad hates it when people are bored. He says the world is so interesting nobody should ever be bored."

"I see," Gloria said, as if she didn't.

"So we'll go see him," Huey said, "and we just won't tell him we're bored. We're bored, but we won't tell him."

"Just so you remember that!" I said.

"Oh, I'll remember," Huey said.

Huey was wearing his angel look. When he has that look, you know he'll never remember anything.

Huey and I put on sweat bands. Gloria put on dark glasses. We started out.

The sun shined up at us from the sidewalks. Even the shadows on the street were hot as blankets.

Huey picked up a stick and scratched it along the sidewalk. "Oh, we're bored," he muttered. "Bored, bored, bored, bored, bored!"

"Huey!" I yelled. I wasn't bored anymore. I was nervous.

Finally we reached a sign:

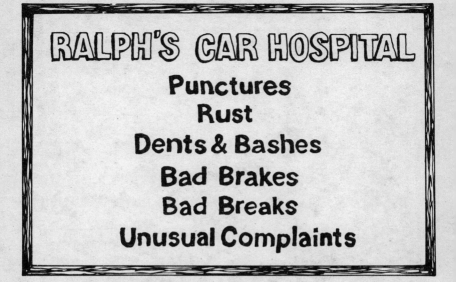

That's my dad's sign. My dad is Ralph.

The parking lot had three cars in it. Dad was inside the shop, lifting the hood of another car. He didn't have any customers with him, so we didn't get to shake hands and feel like visiting mayors or congressmen.

"Hi, Dad," I said.

"Hi!" my dad said.

"We're—" Huey said.

I didn't trust Huey. I stepped on his foot.

"We're on a hike," I said.

"Well, nice of you to stop by," my father said. "If you want, you can stay awhile and help me."

"O.K.," we said.

So Huey sorted nuts and bolts. Gloria shined fenders with a rag. I held a new windshield wiper while my dad put it on a car window.

"Nice work, Huey and Julian and Gloria!" my dad said when we were done.

And then he sent us to the store across the street to buy paper cups and ice cubes and a can of frozen lemonade.

We mixed the lemonade in the shop. Then we sat out under the one tree by the side of the driveway and drank all of it.

"Good lemonade!" my father said. "So what are you kids going to do now?"

"Oh, hike!" I said.

"You know," my father answered, "I'm surprised at you kids picking a hot day like today for a hike. The ground is so hot. On a day like this, frogs wear shoes!"

"They do?" Huey said.

"Especially if they go hiking," my father said. "Of course, a lot of frogs, on a day like this, would stay home. So I wonder why you kids are hiking."

Sometimes my father notices too much. Then he gets yellow lights shining in his eyes, asking you to tell the whole truth. That's when I know to look at my feet.

"Oh," I said, "we *like* hiking."

But Gloria didn't know any better. She looked into my father's eyes. "Really," she said, "this wasn't a real hike. We came to see you."

"Oh, I see!" my father said, looking pleased.

"Because we were bored," Huey said.

My father jumped up so fast he tipped over his lemonade cup. "BORED!" my father yelled. "You were BORED?"

He picked up his cup and waved it in the air.

"And you think *I* don't get BORED?" my father roared, sprinkling out a few last drops of lemonade from his cup. "You think I don't get bored fixing cars when it's hot enough that frogs wear shoes?"

" 'This is such an interesting world that nobody should ever be bored.' That's what you said," I reminded him.

"Last week," Huey added.

"Ummm," my father said. He got quiet.

He rubbed his hand over his mouth, the way he does when he's thinking.

"Why, of course," my father said, "I remember that. And it's the perfect, absolute truth. People absolutely SHOULD NOT get bored! However—" He paused. "It just happens that, sometimes, they do."

My father rubbed a line in the dirt with his shoe. He was thinking so hard I could see his thoughts standing by the tree and sitting on all the fenders of the cars.

"You know, if you three would kindly help me some more, I could leave a half hour early, and we could drive down by the river."

"We'll help," I said.

"Yes, and then we can look for frogs!" Huey said. So we stayed. We learned how to make a signal light blink. And afterward, on the way to the river, my dad bought us all ice cream cones. The ice cream did melt. Huey's melted all down the front of his shirt. It took him ten paper napkins and the river to clean up.

After Huey's shirt was clean, we took our shoes and socks off and went wading.

We looked for special rocks under the water—the ones that are beautiful until you take them out of the water, when they get dry and not so bright.

We found skipping stones and tried to see who could get the most skips from a stone.

We saw a school of minnows going as fast as they could to get away from us.

But we didn't see any frogs.

"If you want to see frogs," my father said, "you'll have to walk down the bank a ways and look hard."

So we decided to do that.

"Fine!" my father said. "But I'll stay here. I think I'm ready for a little nap."

"Naps are boring!" we said.

"Sometimes it's nice to be bored," my father said.

We left him with his eyes closed, sitting under a tree.

Huey saw the first frog. He almost stepped on it.

It jumped into the water, and we ran after it.

Huey caught it and picked it up, and then I saw another one. I grabbed it.

It was slippery and strong and its body was cold, just like it wasn't the middle of summer.

Then Gloria caught one too. The frogs wriggled in our hands, and we felt their hearts beating. Huey looked at their funny webbed feet.

"Their feet are good for swimming," he said, "but Dad is wrong. They don't wear shoes!"

"No way," Gloria said. "They sure don't wear shoes."

"Let's go tell him," I said.

We threw our frogs back into the river. They made little trails swimming away from us. And then we went back to my father.

He was sitting under the tree with his eyes shut. It looked like he hadn't moved an inch.

"We found frogs," Huey said, "and we've got news for you. They don't wear shoes!"

My father's eyes opened. "They don't?" he said. "Well, I can't be right about everything. Dry your feet. Put your shoes on. It's time to go."

We all sat down to put on our shoes.

I pulled out a sock and put it on.

I stuck my foot into my shoe. My foot wouldn't go in.

I picked up the shoe and looked inside.

"Oh no!" I yelled.

There were two little eyes inside my shoe, looking out at me. Huey and Gloria grabbed their socks. All our shoes had frogs in them, every one.

"What did I tell you," my father said.

"You were right," we said. "It's a day when frogs wear shoes!"

THE BET

Gloria and I were in the park. I was in one of those moods when I want to beat someone at something. And Gloria was the only one around.

"Bet I can jump farther than you," I said.

"Bet you can't," Gloria said.

We made a starting line on the ground and did broad jumps.

"I win!" I said.

"But not by much," Gloria said. "Anyway, I jumped higher."

"I doubt it," I said.

"I bet you can't jump this railing." The railing went around the driveway in the park.

"I'll bet," Gloria said.

We both jumped the railing, but Gloria nicked it with her shoe.

"You touched it!" I said. "I win."

"You win too much," Gloria said.

She sat down on the grass and thought.

I sat down too. I wondered what was on her mind.

"Well," Gloria said, "I guess you can win at ordinary things. But I can do something special."

"Like what?" I said.

"Bet you I can move the sun," she said.

"Bet you can't!" I said.

"Bet I can," Gloria said. "And if I win, you have to pay my way to a movie."

"If you lose," I said, "you pay my way. And you're going to lose, because nobody can move the sun."

"Maybe you can't," Gloria said. "I can."

"Impossible!" I said.

"Well—suppose. Suppose I make you see the sunset in your bedroom window? If I can do that, do you agree that I win?"

"Yes," I said. "But it's impossible. I have an east window; I see the sun rise. But the sun sets in the west, on the other side of the house. There's no way the sunset can get to my window."

"Ummm," Gloria said.

"What are you thinking about?" I asked. "Thinking how you're going to lose?"

"Not at all," Gloria said. "I'm thinking about what movie I want to see."

"When are you going to make your miracle?" I asked.

Gloria looked at the sky. There were hardly any clouds.

"Today will be just fine," she said. "Here's what you have to do. . . ."

It was seven o'clock at night. I was in my room. I

had done what Gloria asked. I had pulled the telephone into my bedroom on its long cord.

It was halfway dark in my bedroom. No way the sun was coming back.

The phone rang. I picked it up.

"Hello, Gloria," I said. "The phone isn't the sun."

"Look out your window," Gloria said.

"I don't see anything unusual," I said.

"O.K.," Gloria said. "Now watch your wall, the one across from the window."

I watched. A big circle of yellow light was moving across the wall. It floated higher. Then it zigzagged across the ceiling. Then it floated back down the wall again. It looked just like the sun does coming in the window in the morning. Except the morning sun doesn't dance on the ceiling.

I spoke into the phone. I had to admit—"It looks like the sun!"

Gloria's voice sounded far away. "It *is* the sun. Now look out your window again," she said. "Look at my house."

From the second floor of our house we can see over lots of garages and back yards to the top floor of Gloria's house.

"See my house?" Gloria asked.

"Yes."

"See my window?"

"Yes."

"Look hard!" Gloria said.

And then I saw a person leaning out Gloria's window. It was Gloria. And I saw what she had in her hands—a mirror big enough to move the sun.

"Gloria! You're reflecting the sun into my house!" I said. "You're sending signals!"

It was a wonderful invention! I didn't know exactly what it was good for, but it seemed like it must be good for something.

"Of course!" Gloria said. "I've got to stop now."

The sun went away. Her voice went away. I guessed her arms were getting tired from holding that big mirror out the window.

Then I heard her voice on the phone again.

"Did I do it, or didn't I?" she asked.

"Do what?" I answered. I was so excited about the signaling invention I had forgotten about the bet.

"Move the sun!" Gloria said.

"Yes," I said, "you did it. You win."

"Ummm," Gloria said. Her voice was full of satis-faction.

I knew what she was thinking about—what movie she wanted to see.

And I was thinking how I was going to have to do something I never want to do—at least for years and years and years: pay a girl's way to a movie.

I LEARN FIREFIGHTING

I Wish for
Smokey the Bear

I do not like trouble. Really, I don't understand how I get into it so often when I hate it so much.

I would like to be like Smokey the Bear. I would like to be the person who sees the little spark that starts trouble and puts it out, like a forest fire, right at the beginning.

The trouble is, I don't see the little sparks. That's my trouble.

And I have one other trouble: great ideas.

I was in the back yard with Gloria and Huey. There are two new things in our back yard. One is a swing that is the best in town. My dad used a ladder to hang it in a great big tree.

When I sit in this swing and look straight up, it's like looking to the roof of the world. And when we swing in our swing, we go high and wide—high as the roof of our garage, wide enough so the ropes bend where your hands hold them, and you wonder if you'll somersault by accident.

The other new thing is a sandpile that's as high as a little mountain. Gloria and I build mining towns and rivers and bridges and roads there. We pretend we're digging for gold on the planet Arcturus.

Everything used to be peaceful. We swung a lot. We made a lot of towns in the sandpile. But then one day I got a great idea.

I was swinging. Huey and Gloria were standing by the tree.

I could see the sandpile almost under me. I checked to make sure there were no trucks in it.

Then I pushed off from the swing. It was like flying. There was a minute when I was sitting still in the air. Then it was like parachuting.

I landed in the sandpile. I broke three mines, one road, a bridge, a barbershop, a jail and a bank. But I was fine. I figured we could build the mining town over again.

"All right!" Gloria said. She got in the swing. In a minute she flew too, just like me.

"Your turn, Huey!" I said.

"O.K.," Huey said. He didn't sound very excited.

Huey got in the swing. Very slowly he started to go higher.

"Hurry up, Huey!" Gloria said.

"Just a minute," Huey said. He started to slow down.

"What do you mean, 'just a minute'?" I said. I wanted my next turn.

"Just a minute, I can't do it until I put on my baseball cap," Huey said. He got out of the swing and got his cap from the porch.

"Come on, Huey!" Gloria said.

He got back in the swing and started higher.

"Higher, Huey!" I shouted.

Huey started slowing down again.

"Wait a minute, I need my lucky shirt," Huey said. He meant his Superboy T-shirt.

"No you don't, Huey," I said.

"Well, I can't go until I tie my shoelaces," Huey said.

"Huey, get out if you aren't going to jump," I said.

"No," Huey said, "it's my turn." He was still working on his shoelaces.

"Huey," Gloria said, "you *had* your turn. You just didn't use it."

"I don't like the way you play," Huey said.

"If you don't like it, go play by yourself," I said. "You're a scaredy-cat, anyway," I added. "Who wants to play with a scaredy-cat?"

That was the spark.

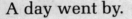

A day went by.

"So, who cares if Huey doesn't play with us?" I said.

"Yes," Gloria said, "who cares?"

But I did care a little. It was inconvenient to play mining town without Huey. Huey had taken his plow, his dump truck and his steam shovel away from the sandpile. He was keeping them on the shelf by the top bunk bed where he sleeps. He was sleeping with his steam shovel at night as if it was his only friend.

On the second day he came out on the back porch and watched us swinging.

"So what are you doing, scaredy-cat?" I said.

That was the second spark.

The next day Huey stayed in our bedroom with the door closed. I could hear thumps from the other side of the door. Once I opened the door. Huey was sitting on the floor.

"What are you doing, Huey?" I said.

"None of your business!" Huey said.

I closed the door again.

When he came to dinner, he didn't look at me.

My mother brought out the food.

"Huey," my mother said, "you have to have some broccoli. It's good for you. It will make you strong."

"All right," Huey said.

He ate three helpings! I couldn't believe it. Usually Huey only pretends to eat broccoli. Usually he stores it in his pants pockets and gets rid of it later.

"May I be excused?" Huey said.

He went upstairs to our room and closed the door again.

My father looked
at Huey's empty chair.

"Seems like something
strange is going on around
here," my father said. He
had those dangerous yellow
lights in his eyes. "Seems like I
haven't seen you and Huey talk
to each other for three days.
Did you two have a fight?"

"Oh no," I said.

"No?" my father repeated.

"Really," I said.

And just then there was a huge crash like a tree
falling above us.

In a second Huey came walking very stiffly down the stairs, like a soldier on parade.

Blood was coming from his nose.

His lip was cut.

One side of his face was swelling.

"Huey!" my mother said. "Are you all right?" She went running to him.

"I'm all right," Huey answered. He kept walking right by us, on his way to the kitchen. "I just need a Kleenex."

"You need more than that!" my mother said. "You need an ice pack! You need a bandage!" She followed him into the kitchen.

"Julian," my father said. "Something tells me this situation has something to do with you."

Superboy

I couldn't say yes.

I couldn't say no.

"Maybe," I said.

"MAYBE?" my father said.

I wished I was a Smokey the Bear person. I wished I knew trouble before all of a sudden I felt it like a fire in my feet, my hands, my heart, my soul, my brain.

and Me

I could hardly see Huey. Huey could hardly see.

He had a Kleenex under his nose. He had a washcloth full of ice against his face. Every now and then he moved the washcloth and an ice cube fell to the floor, rattling like a marble.

We were standing in front of my father and mother.

"So, what *did* you do, Huey?" my father asked, sounding like a judge.

"I—I wanted to be strong," Huey said. "I—I wanted to be Superboy. So I was getting strong. I did sit-ups. I did push-ups. I ate broccoli. I thought I would get tough if I practiced falling out of bed. First I practiced falling out of the bottom bunk. Then I practiced falling out of the top bunk. Once."

"And you're all banged up and you didn't even cry," my mother said.

"Superboy doesn't cry," Huey said. "I am never ever going to cry again."

And right then he started crying.

My mother put her arms around him.

"Huey," my mother said, "everybody cries sometimes. Even Superboy."

"Superboy cries?" Huey said. He stopped crying.

"Huey," my mother said, "why did you want to be Superboy?"

"Julian called me a scaredy-cat," Huey said.

His ice pack slipped. I could see his face turning purple.

"Huey," I said. "I really didn't mean it. I was wrong. You're brave."

And then I cried too.

Huey went up to bed. My mother got more ice and went with him and read him a story.

"Julian," my father said, "you and I are going to have a talk."

We went into the living room.

Pretty soon I had told my side, about the swing and the sandpile and how Huey gets me angry when he acts like a baby.

"I understand how you feel, Julian," my father said. "But there are some things you need to think about."

I waited to hear how I was careless and how I got Huey in trouble. And I waited to hear what punishment I was going to get.

But that's not what my father said.

He said I was a smart boy. And he said Huey needed a smart older brother like me, not just parents, to take care of him. And he said that sometimes it would be hard, but when I am older I will be proud of myself because I helped Huey to grow up and took good care of him.

I didn't know what to say.

Finally I said, "I thought you were going to punish me."

"I don't think you need punishing," my father said. "Sometimes maybe I've punished you too hard."

And then he said the most surprising thing of all.

"Julian, you're learning to be a good older brother. I'm still learning how to be a father too."

Huey Makes
the Leap

"O.K., Huey!" my father said.

"You can do it, Huey!" Gloria said.

Huey had on his lucky T-shirt. He had his shoes tied. He had on his baseball cap. His feet were aimed for the sandpile.

"Bail out!" I yelled.

Huey pushed off from the swing. For a second he floated. I saw his face. He had his eyes shut tight.

In a second he had landed, plunging into the sand, legs straight out in front of him.

"A record!" Gloria said.

"Yes!" I said. "Huey, you went out farther than Gloria or me!"

"Really?" Huey said. "It was fun!"

"More fun than falling out of bed!" my mother said.

"How did you do it, Huey?" Gloria asked. "How did you break our record?"

Huey was in his Superboy pose, with his shoulders back and his thumbs hooked in his belt.

"Yes," my mother said, "what's your secret?"

Huey scuffed his tennis shoes in the sand. "Broccoli," he said.

THE BOX

My mother was at a meeting. And my father had an errand to do.

"Will you kids be all right till I get back?" he asked.

"Sure," we said.

"Fine," my father said. "I may have a surprise for you."

"Great!" I said.

My dad left.

"I wonder what your surprise will be," Gloria said.

"Me too," Huey and I said, both at the same time.

The three of us stayed in the back yard, taking turns swing-jumping. We didn't hear my dad coming back. It started getting dark and hard to see.

"I jumped farther than you," Huey said.

"You didn't," I said.

"Did too," Huey said.

"Did not, bean sprout," I said.

"Did not, WHAT?" my father said. He *had* come home. He was on the porch.

"Just *did not* was all I said."

"He called me 'bean sprout'!" Huey shouted.

"BEAN SPROUT!" my father roared. "He called you BEAN SPROUT?"

"I think I'll be going home now," Gloria said, very softly. She was already in the shadows, halfway out of the yard.

My father stepped out the porch door. He put down a big cardboard box he was carrying.

"Wait a minute, Gloria," my father said. "I'd like you to stay. I have something in mind for these boys!"

I looked at Huey. "We can forget the surprise," I whispered.

"A surprise is coming," Huey whispered back. "But it won't be nice."

We all followed my father into the house.

"Are you going to send us to our room?" I asked.

"No," my father said. He had a scary smile.

"Are you going to make us wash windows?" Huey asked.

"No," my father said. He smiled again, like a tiger.

"What *are* you going to do?" Gloria asked.

"I have an idea about these boys, Gloria," my father said, just like he and Gloria were best friends. "I think they need to go through a potentially dangerous situation together. Then they may like each other more."

"What do you mean, a 'potentially dangerous situation'?" I said.

"I mean one that *could* be dangerous if you don't handle it right." My father smiled again, like a cobra.

"Like what?" Huey said.

"I know you boys like animals," my father said. "It wouldn't be anything much. Something like— live alligators. Maybe—sharks."

"Sharks!" Huey said. He reached for my hand.

"Now you boys make yourselves comfortable," my father said. "Gloria and I will be back in a minute."

The two of them walked outside to the porch. Gloria looked back at us. Her eyes said good-bye forever.

Huey and I sat on the couch.

"Is Gloria going to help carry in the sharks?" he asked.

"I don't know!" I said. "Huey, I'm sorry I called you 'bean sprout.' "

"That's O.K.," Huey said.

"It's taking them a long time," I said.

We waited. Huey started rubbing his special laser ring that is supposed to fry your enemies to a crisp, although actually it couldn't even fry an egg.

Gloria and my father came back. They had the cardboard box my father had left on the porch.

"Hold it level, Gloria," my father said.

Inside the package something skittered.

"Not sharks," Huey whispered to me. "Maybe— live snakes!"

Gloria and my father set the box down in front of us. It was tied with a strong cord. I moved my feet away from it.

"Now your job," my father said to us, "will be to open this box."

"O.K.," Huey said, rubbing his ring.

"I don't want to," I said.

Gloria looked at me sympathetically. Even my father looked a little bit sorry.

"I don't want you to go into this without a fighting chance," he said. "Wait a minute."

He went into the kitchen.

I looked at the box. I tried to sense what was inside it. All I could sense was darkness. And breathing.

"Gloria," I whispered quickly, "do you know

what's inside there? Would you say it's really dangerous?"

"I would say"—Gloria began—"that if I were you, I would say my prayers."

"Well, here you are," my father said cheerily.

He was carrying two kitchen knives.

I started making a plan. Huey and I could stab the box to shreds. Afterward, we could find out what *had been* inside. I picked up one of the knives.

"Sorry," my father said. "The knives are for later. You have to open the box with your bare hands."

"With our bare hands?" Huey repeated. He didn't look so brave anymore.

"Right!" my father said. "And be gentle. That's a good box. I may want to use it again."

"Couldn't this wait until tomorrow?" I said.

Sometimes my father gets over his strange ideas in a day or so.

My father smiled his tiger-cobra smile. He raised his eyebrows.

"No," he said. "But I'll help you a little."

He took one of the knives and cut the cord on the box. That left only a little piece of tape on the top between whatever it was and us.

"Can't you tell us *anything* about what's in there?" I said.

"Just this," my father said. "They're hungry!"

Whatever it was, there was more than one!

"Come on, Julian," Huey said. He was rubbing his laser ring.

"Ready," I said.

We each took hold of one top flap of the box. We

pulled in opposite directions so hard we fell on the floor. Nothing came out of the box at us.

We got up. We moved closer to the box.

"It's the surprise!" Huey said.

In one corner of the box were two baby rabbits. They blinked in the light. Their long ears trembled. One was brown. One was white.

Huey put his hand into the box. The white one smelled it.

"They're brothers," my father said, "and they're hungry."

Huey picked up the white one and held it in his hands.

I picked up the brown one.

"You said they were dangerous," I said.

"Could be," my father said. "If you boys don't

take those knives and cut them some lettuce and carrots, they might start nibbling your shirts."

So we cut up lettuce and carrots while Gloria held the rabbits.

"Well, what about names?" my father said.

I thought of the toughest name for a rabbit I could. "Mine is Jake," I said.

"And what about you, Huey?" my father asked.

"Wait a minute. I have to think," Huey answered. He shut his eyes.

In a minute he opened them. He didn't say anything.

My father said, "Come on, Huey. What is it? Tell us."

Huey got a big grin on his face. "Bean Sprout," he said.

A CURVE
IN THE RIVER

This is something I learned in school: The whole body is mostly water.

We think we're solid, but we're not. You can tell sometimes from your blood and tears and stuff that what you're like inside isn't what you're like outside, but usually you'd never know.

Also, the whole earth is mostly water—three-quarters ocean. The continents are just little stopping places. And using water—streams and rivers and oceans—anybody could put a message in a bottle and send it all the way around the world.

That was my secret project.

I had a bottle with a cork. I had paper and a ballpoint pen. I wrote a message: *Whoever finds this bottle, please write or call me and tell me where you found it.*

I put down my address and phone number. Then I corked the bottle and carried it down to the river.

I threw the bottle as far out as I could. It splashed, bobbed up and floated. I watched it go out of sight.

I kept thinking about my secret project.

Maybe my bottle was on the way to Hawaii.

Maybe it was on the way to France.

Maybe it was on the way to China.

Maybe I would write letters to the person who found it, and we would become friends. I would go visit the person where he or she lived.

I could see myself in Rio de Janeiro, dancing in the streets.

I could see myself in India, riding on an elephant.

I could see myself in Africa, taming wild lions.

A week went by.

I wondered how long I'd have to wait before I heard from the person who got my bottle. It might be months.

Maybe my bottle would go to the North Pole and

be found stuck in the ice by Eskimo hunters. Then I realized it might lie in the ice for years before it was found. Somebody might phone or write me, and I would even have forgotten about my bottle.

I decided I should write a note to myself and hide it in my desk, where I would find it when I grew up, so I could remind myself about the bottle then.

Dear Old Julian, I wrote. *Remember the bottle you threw in the river?* And then I put down the day and the year that I threw it in.

I had just finished hiding this message in the back of my desk when the phone rang.

It was Gloria.

"Julian, I have some news!" she said.

"Oh, really?" I said. Nothing could be important news that wasn't about my bottle.

"Julian," Gloria said, "it's about your bottle with the message—I found it!"

She sounded happy. I wasn't. My bottle was supposed to travel around the world.

"Julian?" Gloria said.

I didn't answer.

All that water to travel! All those countries to see! The whole world full of strangers! And where did my stupid bottle go? To Gloria's house!

"Julian?" Gloria said. "Are you still there?"

I couldn't talk. I was too disgusted. I hung up.

Gloria came looking for me.

"Tell her I'm not here," I said to Huey.

Huey went to the door. "Julian says he's not here," Huey said.

"Oh," Gloria said. She went away.

In a couple of days my father started noticing.

"I haven't seen Gloria lately," he said.

"I don't want to see her," I said.

"Why?" my father said.

"Because."

Then I decided to tell my father about the bottle and how Gloria found it. It didn't matter anymore to keep it a secret. The secret was over.

"That's too bad," my father said. "But it's not Gloria's fault."

"She found the bottle," I said. "She must be laughing at me for trying such a stupid idea."

"It's not a stupid idea," my father said. "You just had bad luck. You know what your problem is? It's the curve in the river. Your bottle got stuck on that curve, and it didn't have a chance."

I felt a little better. I went to see Gloria.

"I wanted to give you your bottle back," Gloria said. Then she added, "I thought it was a great idea, sending a message in a bottle."

"Well, it's a good idea, but it's a no-good idea because of the curve in the river. The bottle couldn't get around it," I explained.

"I guess it couldn't," Gloria said.

"Julian," my father said, "I have to make a long trip in the truck Saturday. I have to pick up some car parts. I'm going to go past the big bridge down the river. Would you like to ride along?"

I said I would.

"You know," my father said, "there's something we could do. We could walk out on the bridge. And if you wanted, you could send a new message. Your bottle would have a good chance from there. It's past the curve in the river."

I thought about it. I decided to do it. And I told my father.

"You know," he said, "if you don't mind my advice—put something special about yourself in the bottle, for the person who finds it."

"Why?" I asked.

"It'll give the wind and the water something special to carry. If you send something you care about, it might bring you luck."

I was working on my new message. And then I

thought about Huey and Gloria. I thought how they might want to send bottles too. It didn't seem so important anymore that I be the only one to do it.

And that's what we did. We all got new bottles, and we put something special in each one. We each made a picture of ourselves for our bottle.

And in his, Huey put his favorite joke:

Where does a hamburger go on New Year's Eve?

To a meat ball.

In hers, Gloria put instructions on doing a cartwheel.

In mine, I wrote instructions for taking care of rabbits.

We added our addresses and phone numbers and

pushed in the corks tightly. We were ready for Saturday.

The bridge was long and silver and sparkled in the sun. It was so big that it looked like giants must have made it, that human beings never could have. But human beings did.

My father parked below the bridge. "From here we have to walk," he said.

We got out of the truck, which always smells a little bit of dust, but mostly of the raisins Dad keeps on the dashboard.

We walked in the outside walkers' lane to the middle of the river. Cars whizzed past. We each had our bottle in a backpack.

The bridge swayed a little. We could feel it vibrate. My father held Gloria's and Huey's hands. I held Gloria's other hand.

"It's scary, but it's safe," my father said.

We held on to the bridge railing and looked over the side. The green water slid under us very fast. For a minute it seemed like the bridge was moving and the water was standing still.

We unpacked our bottles.

"Don't just throw them over the side," my father said. "Make some wishes. Sending messages around the world is a big thing to do. Anytime you do a big thing, it's good to make wishes."

We did.

I don't know what Huey or Gloria wished. I wished our bottles would sail along together. I wished they wouldn't get trapped in seaweed or ice, or hit rocks. I wished we'd make new friends on the other side of the world. I wished we'd go to meet them someday.

"Ready?" my father said.

Together we threw our bottles over the side. They made a tiny splash. They looked very small, but we could see them starting toward the ocean.

They were like Columbus's ships. I hoped they'd stay together a long, long time.

About the Author

Ann Cameron is the bestselling author of many popular books for children, including several Stepping Stones: *The Stories Julian Tells; More Stories Julian Tells; Julian, Secret Agent; Julian, Dream Doctor; Julian's Glorious Summer; The Stories Huey Tells; More Stories Huey Tells;* and *Gloria Rising.* She also wrote *Colibrí,* a *Booklist* Editors' Choice and an ALA Notable Book for Children. Ms. Cameron lives in Guatemala. Visit her at www.childrensbestbooks.com.

Go on more adventures with Julian!

Julian, Secret Agent

A man came toward us. He was the biggest man I ever saw. He must have been practically seven feet tall. He had two huge bags of groceries that he was balancing on his shoulders. He was wearing shorts and a T-shirt that said RAMBO! He had muscles every place on his body that you could have a muscle, and he looked mean.

I pictured myself getting mashed, pictured Dad standing by my bed afterward, shaking his head sadly and saying, "Julian, you went too far."

If you like Julian's stories,
check out the ones his brother tells!

The Stories Huey Tells

Banana Spaghetti was not the way I had imagined it.

It wasn't yellow. It was brown. It wasn't happy. It looked miserable.

It looked worse than turnips, worse than eggplant, worse than a baked fish eye.

"Maybe it's better than we think," Julian said. "When you don't like some stuff, Mom always tells you it's better than you think."

"Will she eat it?" I asked.

"She'll eat it because we made it," Julian said.

"That might not be a good enough reason," I said.

Read more about Julian's friend Gloria in . . .

Gloria Rising

A woman wearing a sky-blue jogging suit got into line behind me. She was holding a cereal box. She smiled at me, and I smiled back.

I decided to show her what a really good catcher I am. I made a wild and daring onion throw.

I missed the catch. The onion kept going, straight for the middle of the baby food castle. The castle was going to fall!